oh, I'd never be without you, Lizzie Bee   M.D.

For my parents, thank you so much!   C.B.

Teddybear Blue copyright © Frances Lincoln Limited 2004
Text copyright © Malachy Doyle 2004
Illustrations copyright © Christina Bretschneider 2004

The right of Malachy Doyle to be identified as the Author of this work
has been asserted by him in accordance with the Copyright,
Designs and Patents Act, 1988.

First published in Great Britain in 2004 by
Frances Lincoln children's Books, 4 Torriano Mews,
Torriano Avenue, London NW5 2RZ
www.franceslincoln.com

Distributed in the USA by Publishers Group West

British Library cataloguing in Publication
Data available on request

ISBN 1-84507-001-1
Set in Bokka Solid

Printed in Singapore

1 3 5 7 9 8 6 4 2

Visit the Malachy Doyle website at
www.malachydoyle.co.uk

Teddybear Blue

Written by Malachy Doyle

Illustrated by
Christina Bretschneider

FRANCES LINCOLN CHILDREN'S BOOKS

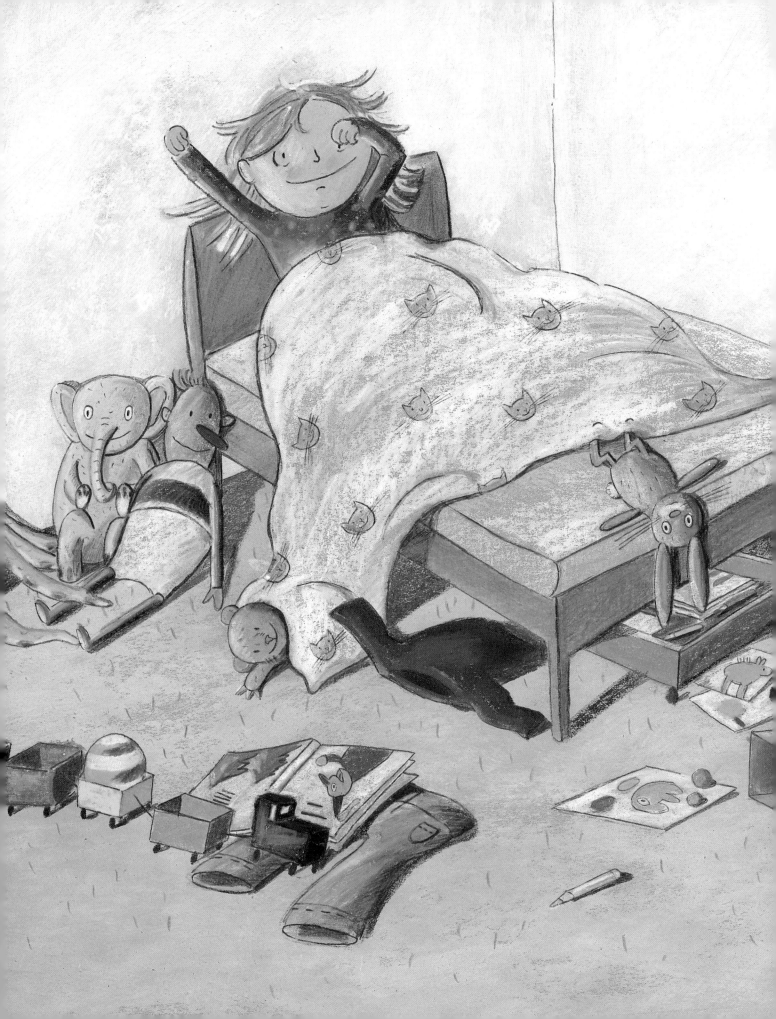

First thing in the morning
he's the one I want to cuddle,
but he's always up before me
and he's hiding in a huddle.
It's the Mummy-Daddy-help-me-
find-my-teddybear blues.

Now you see him,
now you don't.
Now you'll find him,
now you won't.

Now you've got
the disappearing
teddybear blues.

At ten o'clock

we're in the park,

but Teddy's lurking

in the dark.

oh, please will someone
find for me
a teddybear who's...

not always disappearing
when I want him by my side.
Not always running off somewhere

and playing

hidey-hide.

A teddybear who's good,
and not a teddybear who's not.
Not a teddybear who's giving me
the **teddybear blues.**

Yet I **love** him, more than all my other toys put together.

When I'm sad he **always** finds me
and, good or bad, whatever,
he snuggles up beside me
and there's nothing more to do.
oh, I'd never be without you,

Teddy Blue.

You're the one I always choose,
you're the one I hate to lose,

from your fliffy-fluffy haircut
to your funny little shoes.

And that's why we're always singing when we settle down to snooze, the one-and-only, never lonely, teddybear blues.

Oh, I know I say I'll give you
to my sister, **but I don't.**
I know I say I'll find
another teddy,
but I won't.

Because even though you're naughty
when you run away and hide,
there's no one in the world
that I would rather have beside
me in the middle of the night
when I am lonely,
only you.

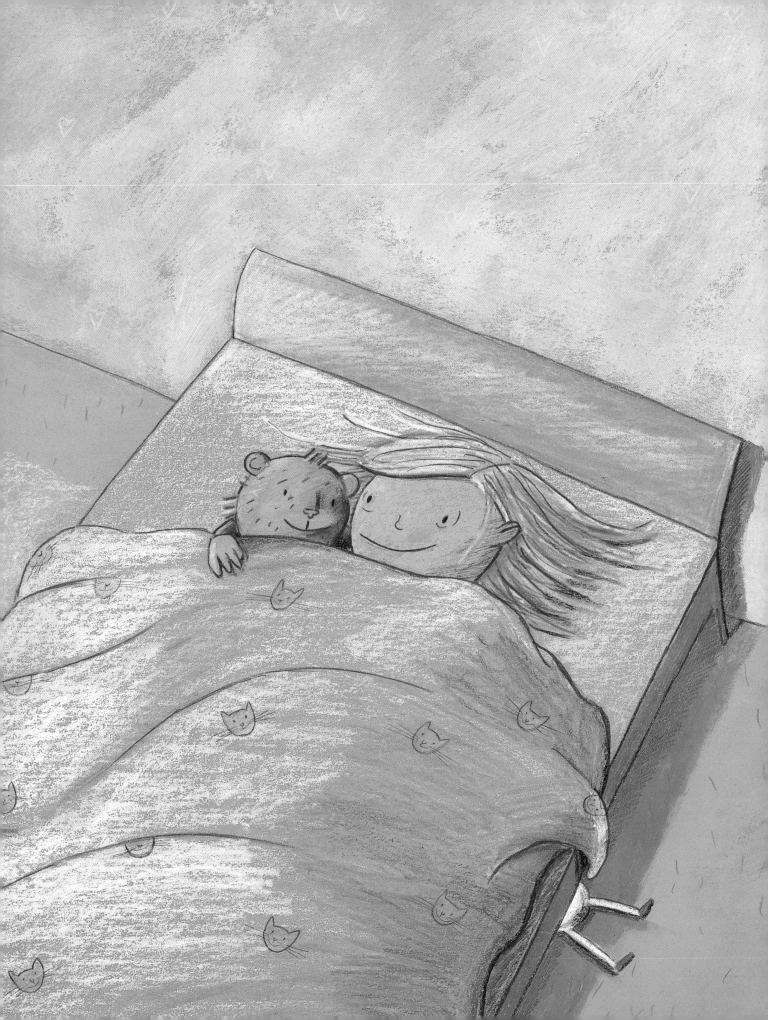

My now-you-see-me,
now-you-don't,
Teddybear
Blue.